AL'S WORLD
MONKEY BUSINESS

AL'S WORLD
MONKEY BUSINESS

BOOK 4

Elise Leonard

ALADDIN PAPERBACKS
NEW YORK   LONDON   TORONTO   SYDNEY

This book is a work of fiction. Any references to historical events, real people, or real locales are used fictitiously. Other names, characters, places, and incidents are the product of the author's imagination, and any resemblance to actual events or locales or persons, living or dead, is entirely coincidental.

ALADDIN PAPERBACKS
An imprint of Simon & Schuster Children's Publishing Division
1230 Avenue of the Americas, New York, NY 10020
Copyright © 2008 by Elise Leonard
All rights reserved, including the right of reproduction in whole or in part in any form.
ALADDIN PAPERBACKS and related logo are registered trademarks of Simon & Schuster, Inc.
Designed by Christopher Grassi
The text of this book was set in Berkeley Old Style.
Manufactured in the United States of America
First Aladdin Paperbacks edition January 2008
10 9 8 7 6 5 4 3 2 1
Library of Congress Control Number 2007933171
ISBN-13: 978-1-4169-3467-7
ISBN-10: 1-4169-3467-7

ACKNOWLEDGMENTS

This book is dedicated to all those people who work with animals:
Zookeepers
Vet Techs
Aquarium Tank Cleaners
Vice Principals
Dog Walkers
Dogcatchers
Chefs
Farmers
Hotel Concierges
Teachers
Etc.

(If I've left out your animal-related job title, I apologize. But I left a
space so you can write it in if you'd like.)

For my readers:
Always use a pooper-scooper.
(A plastic bag will also do.)

For my husband, John:
Can we get a goat?
I know. "Who's going to walk it?"
(You *never* let us get anything good!)

For my sons, Michael and John:
A dog is easier to take care of than a monkey.
But Zeus is easier to take care of than a dog.
(Zeus is our ceramic dog.)

~Elise

AL'S WORLD
MONKEY BUSINESS

CHAPTER

1

"Come on, Al. Knock it off."

I turned around to look at Keith. "Knock what off?"

"I already told you. I have to finish this book by Monday. If I don't, I'll fail English."

"So who's stopping you?" I asked.

"You are," Keith whined.

I couldn't believe he'd said that. "What am *I* doing?"

"Just knock it off, Al. Okay?"

Was I hearing what I was hearing? "Knock *what* off?" I asked.

"Look. I've been working really hard for an hour now. And I have about a hundred more pages to go," Keith grumbled.

"How many pages have you done so far?" I felt for him. I knew if he didn't get his reading done, he *would* fail. Mrs. White, his English teacher, was tough like that.

Keith flipped through his book. "Seven. I've read seven pages."

"In an *hour*?" I asked. I figured after a whole hour, he should have read at least, like, twelve pages.

Keith made gagging noises. "It's not holding my interest. It's supposed to be a *classic*. I keep reading the same three lines over and over."

"So move on to the next line," I advised.

"I tried that. But by then I'm lost because I don't get the *first* three lines," he wailed.

I stomped over to Keith. "Okay. Give me that," I said as I ripped the book from his hands. "Show me where you're stuck."

He pointed. "Right there."

I read the passage to myself.

He was right. It was three lines of really confusing stuff.

"So?" Keith asked.

"So what?" I said.

"So, what do you make of it?"

I shrugged my shoulders. "Beats me. This stuff is drivel."

Keith looked at me. "Don't you mean dribble?"

I handed him back his book. "After reading that, I have no *idea* what I mean."

"See? It's confusing. Right?" he asked.

Usually, Keith's confused by the easiest things. But I had to agree with him on this one. "Yeah," I said with a snort. "It totally blows chunks. I have no clue what it means."

Keith looked like he was going to cry. "Phhw. A classic. Yeah. A classic piece of confusing dribble!"

I patted him on the shoulder. "Well, just skip over that part, and keep reading. Maybe it'll get better."

Keith rolled his eyes. "Yeah. And maybe it won't."

I tried to make him feel better. "Look. Just do it. You've got seven pages done. Just get through the last ninety-seven pages."

"Ninety-three," Keith corrected.

"Whatever. Just do it. It's no fun sitting around here waiting for you."

The park was empty. No one was there. We could've ridden our bikes like maniacs and no one would've seen.

Plus, the day was perfect. Blue sky. Sunny. And a slight wind to cool the sweat off your face.

A perfect Saturday.

I got back on my bike and started to practice my tricks.

After a few minutes, Keith said, "Hey. Knock it off, Al!"

"What? I'm not making any noise," I said honestly. "Stop getting sidetracked, Keith, and just do your stupid reading!"

"Well, maybe I *could*!" Keith hollered back. "If you'd quit throwing stuff at me."

I was practicing my slide stop. You know, stopping while sliding sideways. I always thought that was a very cool move. And I knew I was getting good at it. But I didn't think I was kicking up any rocks or stones or anything.

"I'm not throwing stuff at you, Keith," I said.

"Yes, you are!" he said. He was really annoyed. I could tell.

"Am not!" I countered.

"Yes, you are!" he screamed. "How can I focus

when you keep throwing stuff at me? This stuff is hard enough to learn without getting pelted in the head."

"I'm not pelting you in the head, dude. If I *were* pelting you in the head, you'd *know* it!"

"Well, you *are* pelting me in the head. And I *do* know it!" he screamed. "So knock it off!"

The kid was losing it. He was totally freaking out.

Maybe because the book was too hard or something. He was going postal. And insane.

Just then, out of the corner of my eye, I saw an acorn fly out of the tree Keith was sitting under. It hit him right in the back of the head.

"You're sitting under an acorn tree, you moron," I said to Keith. "Try moving somewhere else."

Keith got up and sat next to a bush. I went back to my slide stop practice.

"You're getting really good at that," Keith said. He was smiling widely and looked impressed.

Of course I was pleased that he'd noticed. But

I really didn't want him to fail English. I felt bad to have to say what I had to say next. But, he's my best friend and it needed to be said.

"Turn around, Keith, and keep reading."

I watched as the smile faded from his face and saw him turn his back to me. "Yeah, okay," he said sadly.

This really stunk. But a man's got to do what a man's got to do. Keith had to read and I had to make him.

I was now practicing my "skid, stop, and sparkling smile while you cross your arms" move. I figured I had the skid and stop down pretty good. Now it was time to add the "sparkling smile and crossing of the arms" part to the end. The whole move would be a killer to the girls. At least it was when Michael Dryden did it.

Michael's really cool and has some really great moves. He goes to our school.

"Get off me, Al," Keith said loudly.

I was practicing the smile and arm crossing

part, so I'd heard Keith loud and clear.

But when I turned around to tell him that I wasn't *on* him, that's when I saw it.

Oh, my God! I thought.

"Don't move!" I said to Keith.

CHAPTER

A l?"

"Yeah, bud?"

"That isn't you, is it?" Keith sounded really scared.

"No. It's not," I said.

"Are you sure?" he asked.

I guess he was hoping. "Not unless I suddenly grew hair all over my body."

"Yeah," Keith said. "Your arms do look really hairy."

I didn't know how to tell him. "They're not my arms, bud."

I saw Keith stiffen with fear. "Are you sure?" he asked.

"Yup. I'm sure," I said.

"Well, if you don't mind my asking, whose arms *are* they?" he asked with care.

I didn't know how to answer him. Mostly because I didn't believe what I was seeing.

"I think it's a troll, dude," I said to Keith.

"Do you think it comes in peace?" he asked.

"It's a gnome, not an alien, Keith." I rolled my eyes.

"Do you see a bridge nearby?" he asked.

I didn't get why he'd ask such a stupid question. But, we were talking about Keith here. Plus, it made me laugh a little. "Why? You want to jump off it?"

"No. I was just wondering if he's far from home," Keith said slowly.

All of a sudden, the troll started squealing and

jumping up and down. Then it started scratching its underarms. If I didn't know better, I'd swear it was a monkey.

Then I looked closer. It *was* a monkey. "Hey. It's a monkey, Keith," I said loudly.

Keith finally turned around. He looked right at the monkey and smiled. "Well, look at that. It *is* a monkey," he said. "Have any bananas, Al?"

"Yeah. I always walk around with bananas on me."

Keith held his hand toward the monkey. "I was only asking. You don't have to get all huffy about it."

I watched as the monkey took Keith's hand. "Hey, look at that! He likes you," I said with wonder. Not that I *didn't* think it would like Keith. I mean, Keith's a likable kind of person. It's just that I'd never seen a monkey make friends before.

"I like him, too," Keith said as he smiled at the monkey.

The monkey started rolling his lips back. He looked like he had on wax lips.

"Hey, he's funny. Isn't he?" Keith asked.

Then the monkey started making loud kissing noises and moving his lips like he wanted to kiss Keith.

"Oh, yeah. He's funny, all right!" I said.

The monkey was blowing kisses at Keith and trying to take Keith's glasses off. "He wants your glasses. Give him your glasses," I said to Keith.

"No way! If I break another pair, my parents said I'll have to buy the next pair myself."

The monkey was getting restless. "Well, give him something, Keith. Can't you tell he wants to play?"

Keith handed over his book.

The monkey took it. He looked at it closely. Then he bit the corner.

I could tell by his face that he wasn't impressed.

He threw the book to the ground and started to jump on it. He stomped his weird-looking feet all over it.

"Yeah. I feel the same way about that book," Keith said to the monkey.

The monkey was really getting into it now. He was screaming loudly and making a big racket. I was afraid someone would notice him.

"Hey, Keith. Quiet him down, would you? If someone sees him, he'll be in trouble," I said.

"Or *we'll* be in trouble," Keith added as he got up to get his book back.

As Keith leaned over to pick up the book, the monkey jumped on Keith. He was hugging and kissing Keith like crazy.

"He's really into you," I said with a laugh.

"I think he's a she," Keith replied.

"How do you know?" I asked.

"I don't know. It's just a feeling," Keith said. The monkey was smacking his—or her—lips at Keith. It looked like it was blowing kisses at Keith.

I laughed again. "Well, then. It looks like you've got a girlfriend there, bud."

Keith rolled his eyes. "Very funny," he said as the monkey kissed him right smack on the lips.

"Or maybe you're married now," I added. "I wouldn't know. I don't speak monkey."

"Come on, Al. This isn't funny."

"It is from over here," I said with a big grin.

The monkey was all over Keith. Hugging and kissing him like there was no tomorrow. Of course, that's when the monkey decided to jump over to me. Right into my arms. Then she started kissing me, too.

I kept my mouth shut and swore I wouldn't open it no matter what!

As the monkey started to pick stuff from my hair, I figured it was safe to speak. "Great," I said.

"Look, Al. She's grooming you. She can't decide who to choose: me or you."

I put my hand over my mouth in case she wanted another smooch. I didn't need monkey germs or anything. "We can't leave her here," I said to Keith from behind my hand. "If someone finds her, they might take her somewhere bad."

"Like where?" Keith asked.

"I don't know! Do I look like I know?" I shouted, forgetting about covering my mouth. It was too late. She planted a big wet one right on me. "Great!" I hollered as I repeatedly spit out all the spit in my mouth. "Just great! Now I'll probably get some rare monkey disease or something!" I muttered to myself. Then I said to Keith, "Look, I have to get my bike to bring it home. So until we can figure out what to do with her, *you'll* have to take her home."

"Why can't she go with you?" Keith asked.

"Because, you moron, I can't take her." Keith could be such an idiot sometimes!

"Why not?" he asked.

"Because it would look stupid riding a bike with a *monkey* on the back," I said. I mean, I had a point. A good point. One I thought was obvious!

"But what if she wants to go with you?" Keith asked.

"Well, it doesn't matter who she *wants*, Keith. She'll *have* to go home with *you*," I said as I pointed to my bike. "Remember? Monkey on back of bike equals . . . no!"

I got on my bike to make my point when I heard Keith blurt out, "She can't come home with me!"

"Why not?" I asked.

Keith looked at the monkey and I could've sworn he looked depressed. "Because my mother's allergic," he said sadly.

I looked at him closely. He'd said some stupid things in his day, but this? This was probably the stupidest thing I'd ever heard him say. "Your mother's allergic?" I questioned.

"Yeah," he said.

"To *monkeys*?" I yelled at him.

"Many people have allergies," he said.

I could tell he was trying to defend his mother. But really! Allergic to *monkeys*? That was just . . . stupid.

"People are allergic to cats, Keith. Or dogs. Maybe trees. Or grass. But *monkeys*?" I shook my head. "I don't think so!"

"She is, Al. My mom's allergic to monkeys. Really!"

It was hard to believe him.

"What do you think?" he said with newfound anger. "You think I made it up?"

"Well, yeah. I do," I said with annoyance.

The monkey jumped on my back and hung on for dear life.

"Why would I make that up?" Keith asked me.

"Who knows?" I screamed. "Maybe so you wouldn't have a monkey on your back. Maybe you don't want to take care of a monkey. How should I know?"

Keith stared at me for a long time. "Are you nuts?" he finally said. "I'd *love* a monkey!"

It was my turn to stare at him.

"It's been a lifelong dream of mine," he said seriously.

I looked at Keith. It was his lifelong *dream*? To have a monkey?

Well, we *were* talking about Keith here. Maybe it

had always been his dream to have a monkey.

"How come you never told me before?" I asked.

Keith shrugged. "I don't know. Maybe I thought you'd think it was . . . silly."

He had a point there.

The monkey must've felt sorry for Keith because she jumped from my back onto his.

"So," I said as I looked at the monkey on Keith's back, "I guess then it's *my* monkey, huh?"

"Looks like it is," Keith said sadly.

He looked like he just found out that the only thing for tonight's dinner was spinach and broccoli.

"*Now* what's the matter?" I asked Keith.

"I wish she was *my* monkey."

I rolled my eyes. Yeah. Right. Like the thing I needed most in my life right now was a monkey.

"Since you get to keep her, can I name her?" Keith asked.

I shrugged. "Yeah, I guess. I don't see why not."

That seemed to cheer him up. "Let's name her George," he said happily.

"*George*? I thought we decided that he was a she?"

Keith smiled crookedly. "Well, yes. We did. But I still want to name her George."

Hey. It was no sweat off *my* nose. What did *I* care? "Yeah, all right," I said to Keith as I looked at the monkey. "But why George?"

"That's the name of the funny monkey from all those books I read as a kid. You know, Curious George. Now *those* were good books," he said as he picked his book up from the ground. He gave it a dirty look. "They say *this* is a classic? No way! Those Curious George books? Now *those* are classics."

CHAPTER

3

So, George," I said to the monkey. "You from around these parts?"

George blew me a raspberry.

"She's a monkey, Al," Keith said with scorn. "Not a cowgirl!"

"Who thought she was a cowgirl?" I asked.

Keith pushed back his glasses with his finger and rolled his eyes. "'*You from around these parts?*' Would you say that to a girl you just met?" He scoffed and rolled his eyes again.

"Excuse me for not knowing proper monkey etiquette!" I screamed at Keith. "But I've never had to pry important info from a *monkey* before!"

"It's not that much harder than talking to a kid," Keith said. Yeah. Like he knew what *he* was talking about.

"If you think you know better, *you* get her to tell us where she's from!" I hollered at him. He could be such a dweezle when he wanted to be. And it seemed like now he really wanted to be.

He was being very protective of the little monkey. If you asked me, he was being over-protective!

"I will! Just watch the master," he said, as he turned his full attention to George. "George?" he asked her.

She scratched her backside and turned away from him.

"George?" he tried again.

She let off a huge round of gas.

"Oh, man," I said as I covered my nose. "Yeah,

you're the master all right," I said to Keith. "You're the master of getting a monkey to cut the cheese! Now *there's* a talent!"

"Oh, be quiet," Keith said as he reached out and turned the monkey so it was facing him. "George. Pay attention. This is important."

George was staring at Keith with her big brown eyes.

"Hmph," Keith said to me. Then he turned back to George. "Where are your people?" he asked her.

"Okay," I said, shoving Keith out of the way. "That's enough. She's not an alien, you dimwit. And she doesn't have 'people.' She's a monkey, you moron!"

Keith looked upset. "Oh, my God. You're right! I hope I didn't offend her."

George grabbed at Keith's glasses again. This time he let her put them on her face.

She grunted loudly once they were on, then puckered up again to kiss Keith.

"She obviously likes your glasses, and *you*, lover

boy," I said to Keith. "You'd better walk home with me so she comes with us."

Keith took her hand in his. "Sure."

We went through the park like that. Me on my bike, Keith walking along next to me, holding George's hand. I was thankful the park was empty.

But we still had to get from the park to my house.

"I'm afraid she's going to get seen," I said to Keith. "Then we'll have to give her up. And who knows *where* she'll end up."

"Yeah," Keith said.

I looked at Keith and George. "You know, I think I have an idea. Isn't there a thrift store right near here?"

"Yes. Right outside the park," Keith said. "Why?"

I sighed loudly. He really wasn't the sharpest tool in the shed. I always had to explain *everything* to him! "If we get her some clothes, maybe we can pass her off as a little kid."

"Hey, that's a great idea!" Keith said.

I already knew that, so I didn't respond.

When we got to the alley behind thrift store, I looked around. We needed to do something with George. But only for a little while. There was a Porta Potti nearby. Ugh. I wouldn't put my worst enemy in one of those. But we had to do something with her. We sure couldn't bring her into the store with us.

Plus, it was a Saturday. I figured, no one was working who would *use* the Porta Potti, so our chances were good that she wouldn't get caught.

"Look, George," I said to the monkey. "I know this is really going to be disgusting for you. But we have to do it. If we don't, they'll take you away from us."

"What do we have to do to her?" Keith asked.

I pointed to the Porta Potti. "No way!" Keith protested. "You are *not* going to put her in there!"

"You have a better idea?" I asked.

I could tell he was thinking about it. "No," he finally said.

So we put her in the Porta Potti after we put

the seat down. We stuck a stick across the out-side handle so she couldn't get out. And then we rushed toward the store.

"We need to get in and get out. Get it?" I asked Keith. "We can't take the chance of someone using that Porta Potti."

"Got it," Keith said, as he opened the store's door for me.

The registers were right near the door. I ran over and asked a checkout lady, "Where's your kid's stuff?"

She pointed toward the middle of the store.

I grabbed Keith and ran toward where she'd pointed. I was in such a hurry, I almost knocked over a whole display.

"Slow down, boys. Settle down. May I help you find something?" a lady asked.

I was just winging it now. You know, off the cuff, so to speak. "I need to get a new outfit for my sister," I said.

Keith snorted a laugh. "Good one," he said.

The lady looked at us like she thought we were nuts or something, but she walked over to some long racks with tiny little clothes. She expected us to follow her. So we did.

"What size is she?" the lady asked.

"About this big," I said as I held my hand about three feet off the floor.

The lady now looked at us like she *knew* we were nuts. "Uh huh," she said, as she nodded and tried not to show how distasteful she found us. She tried, but not very well. Because Keith and I could see she was totally repulsed by us. We *were* kind of sweaty, but maybe she just hates kids.

"And is she thin?" she asked with fake politeness.

I looked at Keith, who shrugged. "No," I said.

"Chubby?" she asked.

That one I knew. "No," I answered.

"Average?" she asked, no longer trying to hide her frustration.

"I guess," I said. I really didn't know if she was

average or not. I didn't know if she was average for a little sister *or* for a monkey. I really didn't know much.

"She's got really long arms," Keith piped in.

The woman nodded. "Remarkably long?"

"Yeah," Keith said. "You could say that."

"Hm," the woman said as she started looking through the racks of clothes. "Okay. I'll keep that in mind."

Encouraged by her words, Keith added, "And she's got *really* short legs. Or as you put it, *remarkably* short."

He looked proud of himself, so he was totally surprised when I belted him in the chest. "Hey! What did you do *that* for?"

"Would you excuse us please?" I said to the lady who looked like she was regretting the moment she first spoke to us.

I pulled Keith out of earshot. "What the heck's the matter with you?" I asked him.

"What's the matter with *me*? What's the matter

with *you*?" he said as he rubbed his chest. "Why'd you go and hit me like that?"

"Because you're making my sister sound like a freak!" I hissed at him.

He rubbed his chest some more. "I'm sorry, Al, but if we don't get the right size, she'll *look* like a freak."

I hated to destroy whatever fantasies he was playing in his head, but I had to do it. "Keith. I'm sorry to have to be the one to tell you this. But I think we've got that whole thing covered already. A monkey wearing kids' clothes is going to look like a freak no matter *what* we pick out. Period. It's a *given*, Einstein."

Keith looked confused. "Well, if you feel that way, then what were you all mad about?"

I shrugged. "I don't know. I didn't like that you were making her *sound* like a freak!"

"Sorry, Al," he said, as the lady came over to us holding out an outfit.

"I think this will look cute," she said as she held

up a red-and-white striped outfit with a matching red hat.

"We'll take it," Keith said quickly, before I had a chance to say anything. "Where do I pay for it?" he asked.

Great. My "little sister" was going to look like a freakish, hairy, little *Where's Waldo*!

CHAPTER

Pink ticket items are fifty percent off today," the lady said.

Keith paid because I never have any money.

"Wow," he said as he held up the top of the outfit. "Can you believe our good luck? I mean, fifty percent off! What a deal!"

"I think there's a reason for that," I said as I looked at the tiny shirt with the arms that hung two feet longer than the body part. Then Keith held up the pants, which were about half the

length of the arms. It was like a . . . what did they call those things? Manufacturer's seconds or something like that. Only usually, the product was still made to fit humanoids. *This* thing looked like it was designed for an orangutan! Or a gorilla. Or . . . a monkey.

A basket piled with used sunglasses sat next to the checkout stand. Most of them were scratched or bent, and some only had one earpiece part. But I grabbed a complete pair that weren't scratched and looked like they would fit George's big head. They had huge round red rims.

"Those will go nicely with your little sister's outfit," the saleslady said as she made eyes with the checkout clerk.

I knew what those eyes meant. They shouted, "Get a load of these two imbeciles!"

The checkout lady looked back at her and gave her a look. *That* look said, "I can't believe we finally got some numbskulls to buy this hideous outfit!"

I looked at Keith. He was completely oblivious.

He was just standing there, forking over his money, smiling like an idiot!

"She's going to love this," he said as we rushed to the Porta Potti. "And the sunglasses? That was brilliant!" he added as he pushed his own glasses up on his nose.

The stick was still across the handle, so we knew she was still in there. *And* that no one had found her.

Now came the hard part.

I'd never dressed a monkey before. I hoped she was in a good mood.

Once my mother was babysitting and she had to change this two-year-old's outfit. Talk about a screaming, squirming mess! He kicked and twisted so much, I figured there was no *way* my mother was going to get the little bugger into his clothes. She had to tickle his belly and bite on his toes. But she finally got the thing dressed.

All I could say was, if we had to go through *that* with George, there was no way on *earth* I was going

to bite her toes! She had some freaky-looking feet!

"You dress her," I said quickly.

"Why me?" Keith asked.

"Because *you're* the one who always dreamed of having a monkey!" That seemed to make sense.

Keith shrugged. "Okay."

George was so excited to see us, she started jumping up and down and screeching.

"No, no, no," I said as I tried to shush her.

"You have to be quiet, George," Keith said.

"Quick," I said. "Give her the glasses."

Keith handed her the sunglasses. She calmed right down and smiled widely.

"Hey, look. You can see all her teeth," Keith said.

That got me thinking. I hoped she didn't bite him while he was trying to dress her.

Keith started with the top. That went on pretty quickly. Although getting her long arms in the sleeves was a bit weird.

"Do one at a time," I said to Keith. "That way

she can play with her glasses with the free hand."

"Good idea," he said.

He tried that, and it worked.

The pants were somewhat harder to put on.

"One leg at a time, Keith," I said.

He tried that, too. It took a while. But finally? Success.

Of course, it was like trying to dress squiggly Jell-O. But like I said, in time, we got it done.

"So now what?" Keith asked.

"We walk her home," I said.

"Cool," he said as he took her hand.

I rolled my eyes. Yeah, right. Cool. How were we going to get her past my mother? My father was no problem. You could parade *twelve* primates dressed like candy canes right in front of the man and he wouldn't notice a thing. But my mother? She noticed *everything*!

"Hey, Keith," I said.

"What?" he asked as he walked along swinging George's weirdly long arm back and forth.

"I need some quarters," I said.

"What for?" he asked.

"I need to get my mom out of the house and I have an idea," I said.

Keith was laughing as he swung George's monkey arm back and forth. "Isn't she cute?" he asked.

I rolled my eyes. "Yeah. Adorable. Now am I getting those quarters or not?"

Keith reached in his pocket with his free hand and took out some change.

We passed a pay phone and I put the money in.

"Hello?" my mom said.

"Mom. It's me."

"Oh hi, honey. Where are you? Still at the park?"

I felt bad for doing it, but I had to lie. "Yeah. Look. This little girl got lost at the park."

"Oh, that's too bad," my mother said. "Is she someone you know?"

"Yeah, she's Hadfaff's little sister," I said. I'd sort of coughed and fake sneezed when I said the name. So it wasn't familiar.

I mean, I was lying to my mother, but I didn't have to involve anyone *else* in the lie.

"Okay, Al," she said.

"Can you do me a favor?" I asked her.

"Sure, honey. What?"

"Can you go to the store and get me some paper for my notebook?"

"Notebook paper? With the three holes?"

"Yeah," I said. "I really need some for school."

"Sure, honey. I'll get it tonight. After dinner."

That wasn't good. "Can you get it now?"

"Now?"

"Yeah, I need it for some homework. And I want to do it as soon as I get home."

I could hear my mother shrug. "Okay, honey. I'll get it now."

Whew. That was close.

I just hoped she didn't go to my room. If she looked in my closet, she'd find a huge pile of notebook paper. All the extra kept piling up every year.

Hey, it wasn't *my* fault that I was efficient in

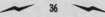

school. I was known schoolwide for my concise reports. My social studies teacher once mentioned that *my* reports were passed all around the faculty lounge. I always assumed they were used for morale.

"Why did you lie to your mom?" Keith asked.

He knew about my closet.

I rolled my eyes. "So she'll be out of the way when we get George to my house."

CHAPTER
5

It was one thing getting my mom out of the house. It was another thing getting George home. That was harder. Much harder.

Not to mention embarrassing.

"I think she looks cute. Don't you?" Keith asked me.

I looked down at the monkey in the middle. "Yeah. I guess."

She kept playing with her sunglasses and laughing. At least I *think* she was laughing. I don't speak monkey, so I wasn't really sure.

"Oh, no," Keith said with a groan.

I looked at Keith and then followed his eyes.

He was looking straight ahead.

"Oh, no," I agreed.

"You think he saw us?" Keith asked.

Since the object of our concern was pointing at us and laughing, I'd have to say yes. "Yeah, it's a safe bet," I replied.

"Dang," was all Keith said.

Dang? That was all he could come up with? Dang? Chad Lavario was headed our way—pointing and laughing. And all Keith could come up with to say was "dang"?

Everyone knew Chad Lavario was the snottiest kid in school. Plus, he never let things drop. He'd see someone walking with a monkey, and before you know it, the whole *school* would know about it.

This wasn't good! Not good at all!

"Is that your *girlfriend*, Alphonse?" he asked as he stopped right in front of us.

He'd said "girlfriend" real snottily. And he made

my name sound like I was a doofus or something.

Before I had a chance to reply, Keith spoke up.

"We don't date monkeys. Do *you*?" Keith said.

I knew he was trying to be as snotty as Chad, but it only sounded childish. And stupid.

Chad scoffed and then snorted a laugh. "You losers don't date at *all*! So a monkey would be a step up," he said with an added snort.

George obviously took offense at that (as did I) and started screeching and howling and trying to get at Chad.

"Hold her tight, Keith," I shouted over George's theatrics. "If she gets loose, she'll rip his eyes out!"

All of a sudden, Chad didn't seem so high and mighty. He was running away like a scared rabbit, screaming like an idiot.

As soon as he rounded the corner, we all started laughing, George included.

"That guy thinks he's so tough. What a wuss!" Keith said as he held his stomach with his free hand.

"Did you see his *face*?" I asked as I, too, doubled over with laughter.

George kept jumping up and down and screeching. Only this time it was with glee, not anger.

"You're pretty smart, aren't you, George?" I asked her.

She curled her lips up and out, and started making smacking kissy noises.

A couple of people were standing nearby and stared at us. They kept their distance, but they were near enough to see we were holding hands with a monkey.

"Come on, Keith," I said. "We'd better go."

Keith got ahold of his funny bone, and we kept walking.

After a while, I decided to walk my bike. So I held George's hand in one hand and my bike in the other.

George got the notion to swing between us. So there we were, walking down the street, and every third step, we'd lift her up and yell, "Wheeeeee."

She'd swing forward and backward and then land on her feet again. Then we'd take three more steps and lift her up and yell, "Wheeeeee."

She was having a blast. I would never admit it out loud, but I was having fun too.

Going down my block should've been tricky, but everyone was either inside or in their yard doing yard work. So no one paid any attention to us.

When we got to my house, I saw my mom's car was not in the driveway or garage. So I knew she was out. But my dad's car was in the driveway.

"You stay here with George," I told Keith. "I want to see where my dad is."

I dropped my bike and quickly ran around to see where he was. Good. He was in the backyard, mowing the lawn.

I ran back to Keith and George. "Quick. Get her upstairs to my room," I said.

We ran through the house, all but dragging George.

She did pretty well with the stairs. Better than

Keith. Keith tripped a couple times as the three of us tried to run up the stairs together.

When we got to my room, we ran inside and closed the door. Then I locked it.

"So now what are we going to do?" Keith asked.

Why did he always think I had all the answers? It was tough always being the smart one.

And for some strange reason, we seemed to find ourselves in tight situations a lot. But it was always *me* who had to find our way out of things.

"I don't know," I said to Keith in answer to his question. "Let me think, would ya?"

I sat down on the corner of my bed to think.

I would have done a lot better, but George kept jumping up and down on my bed. I was jiggling all over the place.

"I'd think better if I weren't getting my brains shaken up," I said to Keith. "Can't you do something with her while I'm trying to figure something out?"

Keith looked at the bouncing monkey. "Well, what should I do?" he asked.

That was it. I'd had enough! "Do I have to think of *everything* around here? Come on, Keith! I can't do this alone!"

I got off the bed because my neck was starting to hurt from all the jolting.

"Maybe she's hungry," Keith said. "I mean, *I'm* hungry. Aren't you?"

He had a point. I was starving. And I knew the last time *I* ate.

I wondered how long ago George last ate. "She might be really hungry," I said more to myself than to Keith.

"What should we make for her? You think she'll eat a sandwich?" Keith asked.

I tried to remember if I'd ever seen a movie or a photo of a monkey eating a sandwich before. As far as I could recall, I'd never seen one. Then I tried to think if I've even *heard* of a monkey eating a sandwich. Nope. Nothing came to mind.

Bananas. That's all I could see. Bananas.

"Hang out here, okay?" I asked Keith. "Let me

go downstairs and look in the kitchen. I hope I find some bananas. 'Cause that's the only thing I can think of to give her."

"What if you don't have any bananas?" Keith asked.

There was a good chance of that. Bananas came and went pretty quickly in my house. They lasted two, maybe three days, tops. After that? They became banana bread. My dad wouldn't eat a bruised banana, so my mom just turned them into bread. They were either sitting there, green, forever, then two days of ripeness, then . . . bread. The natural lifespan of a banana in the Netti household was about the same as that of a tsetse fly!

"Just to be safe, let's go online and see what monkeys eat. I don't think we have any bananas in the house. At least, they weren't here this morning."

"Good thinking," Keith said as he walked over to my computer.

I started the computer and we waited for it to

boot up. All those games I kept on it took forever to load.

When it finally was ready to do something, I clicked to get online.

That took a while too.

CHAPTER

"So what are we doing?" Keith asked.

"I'm going to google 'monkey diet' and see what it says."

Keith looked impressed. "'Monkey diet.' Very good choice," he said.

I rolled my eyes. "Well, I *could* look up 'monkey food' but that seems less, you know, scientific."

When the Google page came up, I was totally confused.

"What's the matter?" Keith asked.

"Well," I said as I read through all the listings. "It says here that monkey diets are richer in vitamins and minerals than human diets."

"What does that mean?" Keith asked me.

I shot him a look. "I don't know!"

"Well, what else does it say?"

I looked down the list. "It seems that different types of monkeys eat different things."

"Like what?" Keith asked.

I looked at the list. "Well, there's the savanna monkey diet. The squirrel monkey diet. The tonkin snub-nosed monkey diet. The yellow-tailed woolly monkey diet. The spider monkey diet. And that's just on this page."

"Well, what do they say?" Keith asked.

That ticked me off. "Don't you think we should know what *kind* of monkey she is first?" I yelled. Okay. So I was getting a little frustrated. I didn't think this would be so hard.

Keith was staring at George. Like that helped.

"Some monkeys eat berries, insects, and leaves. Some eat fruit and seeds. Some eat mostly bamboo leaves," I said as I looked over the Google page.

"Doesn't your mother have a bamboo plant in the living room?" Keith asked.

He looked so excited, I hated to tell him. "It's fake."

"It is? It looks so real," he commented.

I rolled my eyes. "Would you forget the stupid bamboo plant? *We have to figure out what to feed our monkey!*" I hollered.

Now *there* was a sentence I never thought I'd ever say!

I kept reading the Google page. "It says here that the yellow-tailed woolly monkey is primarily frugivorous."

"What the heck does that mean?" Keith asked.

I looked at him. "I don't know! Do I *look* like I know? If I *knew*, don't you think I'd look for some frugivor or something?"

"What's frugivor?" Keith asked. He was getting into it now.

"I . . . don't . . . *know!*" I screamed.

George was getting excited. She was jumping up and down like a maniac and starting to screech again. But not happy screeching. Upset screeching.

"Now look what you've done!" I said to Keith. "You've upset George!"

"How come?" he asked. He looked concerned.

"Because we're *arguing*, you idiot!"

I figured it was best to just bring up a bunch of stuff and see what she ate. I figured she'd eat what she liked. And wouldn't eat what she didn't like.

I brought a whole armload of stuff.

She liked mayonnaise. But didn't like pickles. She ate a whole block of Vermont sharp cheddar before I got a chance to slice it for her. She didn't seem to mind.

She definitely didn't like bologna. She took

the slice I gave her, bit into it, spit it out on my bed, and threw thc rest of the slice at the wall.

It hit the wall with a loud slap. It was kind of funny. It stuck to the wall like it had wallpaper paste on it or something.

When Keith and I cracked up, George snatched the package of bologna. She started pulling out slices of bologna and throwing them like Frisbees across my room.

Slap, slap, slap, slap, slap. Before I knew what was going on . . . I had bologna stuck all over my room! Ceiling included!

Keith was laughing so hard, he fell off the bed.

"Would you knock it off?" I said to him. "And stop encouraging her!"

Keith kept on laughing.

"You're not the one who'll have to clean up this mess!" I said. Then I thought about that. "On second thought. Yes. You *will* have to clean it up."

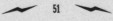

That got him to stop laughing. Pretty quickly! "How come *I* have to clean it up?"

"I'm watching her and letting her stay here. *You* have to clean up after her!"

He didn't look like he was buying it.

"It's only fair," I said.

He nodded slightly. "All right."

As soon as he peeled the last piece of bologna off the ceiling, he said he had to go home.

"Okay," I said. "But come back tomorrow. Early! So we can figure out what to do with George."

"Okay," Keith said. Then he looked at George. "Have fun tonight, you guys."

He looked so sad and lonely, I had to say *something*. "Oh, yeah. It'll be a real pajama party here."

"Darn my mother's allergies!" he muttered as he closed my bedroom door behind him.

Shortly after Keith left, my mom came home from the store. I rushed downstairs so she wouldn't come up.

"Thanks, Mom. I can't tell you how much I needed this," I said with my biggest smile.

"It's okay, dear," she said. "I'll call you when dinner's ready."

"I'm going to start my homework right away. And I had a snack when I came home with Keith. So I don't think I'll be hungry. Why don't you guys eat without me? I'll be working through until bedtime. Then I'll probably crash. So don't disturb me, okay, Mom? It's a hard project and I want to stay focused."

"Okay, dear," she said as she started unpacking some groceries.

"By the way, did you get any bananas?" I asked.

"No. Why?"

"Just checking. I had a craving for them. That's all," I said.

She nodded. "You must be low in potassium," she said. "I'll pick some up tomorrow."

"Thanks, Mom." I was almost at the staircase when I thought to say, "Oh, and if you hear any strange noises coming from my room . . . that's just my research videos and stuff. For my project."

"Okay, dear," she called to me.

"So just ignore any strange noises you hear," I said to make sure she understood.

"Got it," she said.

When I got back to my room, I noticed the mayonnaise jar was completely empty.

I looked at George.

She looked at me.

"You feel okay?" I asked her.

Yeah. Right. Like I was going to get an answer.

I just hoped she didn't have monkey diarrhea all over my room. That was a *lot* of mayonnaise.

Since I was stuck in my room for the rest of the night, I turned on the TV. You know, to keep occupied. I had a little thirteen-incher I'd bought with my birthday money years ago.

Suddenly there was a knock.

"I'm doing homework, Mom!" I called to the door.

"It's me," Keith said. "My mom said I could sleep over. Your mom said it's okay."

I unlocked the door and Keith slipped into the room. Then I locked it again.

He threw his backpack on the floor. "So what are you guys doing?" he asked.

"Watching TV," I said as I jumped on my bed.

I flipped through the channels. When *Teletubbies* came on, George went bonkers.

Of course I flicked right by it, but George ran back to the television and started pointing to the screen. There was mostly news on at that time, so I kept flipping. But when I'd circled around to *Tele-tubbies* again, George went nuts.

"Okay. Okay. We get it," I said to George. "You want to watch *Teletubbies*."

Once George realized that we'd leave it on *Tele-tubbies*, she was all happy.

She hopped on back to my bed and actually snuggled next to me. Great.

Keith nestled in on her other side.

Perfect. Just perfect. I was sitting on my bed. With another guy and a monkey. Snuggling. While we watched *Teletubbies*.

What a weird show!

"I don't get this program at all," I said out loud.

George looked up at me and gave me a raspberry.

Well, I guess *she* showed *me*!

CHAPTER

"Good night, guys," my mom called through the door.

"'Night, Mom," I said.

"Good night, Mrs. Netti," Keith called back.

George let out with a scream.

"What was that?" my mom asked.

"The TV," I said. "We're taking a homework break."

"Okay," she said back. "I'll see you guys in the morning."

Keith picked up his backpack.

"I'm hitting the bathroom," he said. "I'll be right back."

I just looked at him. "Is it my turn to watch you? I didn't know."

He made a face. "Just lock the door behind me."

"Oh," I said. "Right."

Three minutes later there was a knock at my door. "Let me in," Keith said.

I let him in.

Then I cracked up. "What the heck are you *wearing*?!"

"Pajamas," he said simply. "Grams sent them to me."

I stared at him, my grin firmly in place. "You look like a giant banana."

"Good. Maybe George will like *me* better."

I rolled my eyes. "Whatever. But you still look like an idiot."

It hurt my eyes to look at his bright yellow satin outfit.

"Oh yeah?" he asked. "And what are *those*?" He was pointing to my slippers. "Eskimo shoes?"

I took offense. "My *mom* got them for me," I said. "And they feel nice inside. Warm and fuzzy."

Keith made a face. "Look. I won't say anything about your elf shoes, if you don't say anything about my . . ."

I cut him off before he could finish. "Banana suit?" I finished for him.

He didn't treasure the humor.

"I'll take the floor," he muttered as he threw his pillow down.

"Well, you weren't getting the *bed*," I said with a chuckle.

George had chosen a small area at the foot of my bed to mark as her own. She took some of my clothes out of my dresser and bunched them up in lumps and then climbed on top of the pile and fell asleep.

I had to admit, she looked pretty cute.

In the middle of the night I had to go to the

bathroom, and walked in the dark. Once I was done, boy, did I get a surprise! In came George.

She put down the seat, pulled down her red-and-white striped pants and sat like a little lady on the toilet.

She made a tinkle!

Not knowing what I should do (if anything), I wadded up a bunch of toilet paper for her.

Then she looked up at me with her big brown eyes.

I shrugged and said, "I think you should wipe." Then I left the room. You know, so she'd have some privacy.

When I heard the toilet flush, I waited outside the bathroom. I thought I should walk her back to my room. I didn't want her walking into my parents' room by mistake. Or worse, the kitchen.

That's all I needed: for my mother to find a kitchen full of bologna stuck on all four walls.

But she'd walked as quietly as a mouse back to my room, so everything was okay.

In the morning, I explained that she needed to stay quiet while Keith and I went downstairs for breakfast.

She didn't listen.

"You left your TV on," my mom said.

"Yeah," I mumbled. "Sorry."

My dad had his nose stuck in the Sunday paper. "It's kind of loud. Isn't it?" he asked.

"Yeah. Sorry," I said again.

I looked at Keith and grimaced.

He made a face and shrugged.

My dad shuffled the newspaper. "Perhaps you should get back up there," he said softly.

I nodded. "Good idea, Dad."

It was like he knew about George somehow. I didn't know how, though. His face was still buried in the newspaper.

While my mother washed the dishes, Keith and I grabbed some food and brought it upstairs.

"Here you go, George," I said as I held out a blueberry muffin.

"She likes it!" Keith said. "Give her another one."

After that she ate some Fruity Ohs cereal. Dry. Then she took a few sips of half-and-half. But she didn't like that so much.

I'd tried to grab the milk, but the container was too big for me to carry without my parents noticing.

I figured, George is a monkey. What does she know from milk or half-and-half? They're both white!

Keith was having a blast. He was wearing the biggest smile I think I ever saw on him. Maybe it *was* true. Maybe his lifelong dream *was* to have a monkey.

I looked at Keith and smiled. George was grabbing at Keith's glasses and pulled them off.

"Careful with those," he warned George.

George jumped off Keith and ran to the other side of the room.

When she found what she was looking for, she

ran back to Keith and jumped on him again. She held out her round red sunglasses to him.

"Those are yours," Keith said. He pried his glasses from her long fingers. "These are mine."

He put his glasses on and laughed. "She sure has a thing about glasses."

I shrugged.

"So what are we going to do today?" Keith asked.

I'd been thinking about that on and off all night. "I think we should bring her to the zoo. See if she recognizes anyone."

Keith looked at George. "I guess that's a good idea."

He didn't look convinced.

"Keith," I started. "What if *you* got lost and didn't know how to get home?"

Keith looked down at the floor. "Yeah, I guess. Maybe she misses her friends."

I knew that was Keith's way of saying that he'd miss me if *we* got separated. And, well . . . I'd miss him too.

"We'd better get there early, before the crowds," I said.

Keith nodded silently. Then, slowly, "Okay."

"Do you have enough money for three tickets?" I asked him.

"Three?"

"We'll have to pay for a ticket for George. Just in case we have to bring her back out."

That cheered him up. "Yes. I've got enough for three."

So we waited for my mother to go to her room to get dressed, and then we took off.

We played *one, two, three, wheeee* the whole way to the zoo.

It might have been easier taking the bus, but we figured we'd never get George to pass for a little girl on the bus. Three kids walking down the street were basically ignored. But two guys and a monkey on a bus? That might attract some attention.

Keith bought the tickets while George and I hung around the water fountain.

Then the three of us waltzed right past the entrance guard who was flirting with some lady. We'd held the tickets in front of George's face in case the guard was paying attention. But thanks to the pretty lady, we didn't even have to do that.

After that, the place was pretty much deserted.

We went to the elephants and the bears first. Only because those were Keith's and my favorites.

If we got to the monkey house and George made a fuss, we knew we'd get kicked out. So that's why we visited our favorite sections first.

George seemed to really like the elephants. The bears? Not so much.

CHAPTER
8

When we got to the monkey house, George was having a blast. But we didn't think she knew anyone.

"What about that one?" Keith asked. He was pointing to a distant monkey who was staring at George.

I tapped George's shoulder. "Look, George," I said as I pointed to the staring monkey.

Nothing. No response.

Well, a little bit of interest. But you could tell

the other monkey wasn't her long lost uncle Ned or anything.

If that were the case, she'd try to get to him. Right?

"I don't think she's from here."

"So now what?" Keith asked.

"I don't know. But we've got to keep her out of my house as long as possible."

"So where should we take her?" Keith asked.

I felt myself smile as soon as I thought of the perfect plan.

Yes. It was perfect. "Follow me," I said to Keith.

We walked down back alleys. I didn't want anyone seeing George and reporting us.

When we finally got to where we were going, I asked Keith for money.

"How much?" he asked slowly.

"I'm not rolling you in the alley, Keith! I need the money!"

"For what?" he asked.

I knew I'd have him totally on board once I let him know my plans. "Want to see the new Vin Diesel movie?"

"*Yeah!*" he said with great excitement.

"Well, fork over enough for three tickets."

He was reaching into his pocket as I spoke. "Sure thing. Cool."

"Yeah. It's the perfect plan, isn't it? It's a dark place. We can be in there for hours. And no one will even *notice* George," I explained.

"And we get to see a Vin Diesel movie. Cool," he said.

I knew he'd like the plan.

"Let's get the tickets," Keith said. He was heading for the theater entrance.

"Whoa, dude. Hold your horses a minute. We can't wait for tickets together," I said as I grabbed his arm to stop him.

"Why not? We always do."

He was such an idiot. "Not with a *monkey*, we don't, Einstein!"

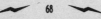

"Oh. Right." He was smart enough to look embarrassed by his mistake.

"You guys wait here and I'll get the tickets. Then I'll come back and get you. We'll sneak in like we did at the zoo."

Keith nodded. "Okay. Sounds like a plan."

When I came back with the tickets, Keith was laughing.

"What's so funny?" I asked him.

"This reminds me of one of my favorite jokes. From when I was a kid."

I waited to hear the joke, but he didn't say anything. Finally I said, "Are you going to tell me or not?"

Keith was still chuckling.

I waited.

He held up his hand as if to say he'd be with me in a minute.

If we hadn't had to wait outside for about fifteen minutes before the show started, I would've been ticked off. But we had to wait outside for fifteen minutes before the show started, so I waited.

"There was this guy," Keith started. "A truck driver. And his job that day was to deliver a whole truckload of penguins to the zoo." Keith started laughing again.

Personally, I didn't see what was so funny. "And?" I asked, figuring there had to be more.

"And his truck broke down." Again, Keith was cracking up.

"*So?*" I asked.

"So he stopped another truck driver and said, 'I'll give you five hundred dollars if you take these penguins to the zoo.'"

Keith was howling now. And George was getting all riled up too. She was screeching and jumping up and down. Having herself a great ol' time.

"So the first truck driver gets his truck fixed. And he's driving back through town. When all of a sudden he sees the *second* truck driver. The guy's waiting in line with a whole row of penguins lined up after him. At the . . . movie theater!"

Keith was laughing again, so I just waited.

"So the first truck driver says to the second truck driver, 'I thought I gave you five hundred dollars to take those penguins to the zoo?!' He was really mad and confused. But mostly mad. Because he didn't want to get fired," Keith explained.

I nodded because I got that part.

"And then the second truck driver says to the first truck driver, 'I *did* take them to the zoo. But I had money left over, so I figured I'd take them to the movies.'"

With that last line out of his mouth, Keith started laughing so hard he couldn't stand up straight. George also thought it was hilarious, because she was jumping up and down and making loud, rowdy monkey noises.

I didn't know how to tell Keith that his and George's reaction to the joke was funnier than the joke itself. So I just laughed at their antics.

We hung out and joked around for the next ten minutes. And then it was time to sneak into the movies.

This time we didn't have a pretty girl to distract the ticket taker. But the crowd was really large. So we just shoved George between the two of us and shuffled in as we waved our three tickets at the teenager in charge.

We rushed George into the theater and found seats.

The theater was pretty crowded. But because this was the first day the movie was released, the multiplex was showing it in two theaters.

We knew everyone would go to the second theater. Because they'd figure the first would be filled up. So we went to the first theater.

"Go check to make sure this one is less full," I told Keith.

He came back a minute later. "Just like always— this theater's not as packed as the other one."

But it was still pretty packed.

Needless to say, the movie was great! A Vin Diesel movie is always a great movie.

Keith bought us some popcorn and Milk Duds. We figured they would keep George quiet.

But she didn't really like the popcorn much.

She preferred the Milk Duds.

If you ever want to see something funny, just watch a monkey eating Milk Duds. The whole caramel experience is a riot. Especially for a first timer. I didn't know a monkey could open its mouth that wide!

Once she was done with those, she became interested in the popcorn. But not to eat. She kept grabbing some and winging it all around the theater.

If we'd gone to see some old-person movie, we would've heard some griping. But this was a Vin Diesel movie. No one cared that they were getting pelted with popcorn. For most people at this movie, it kind of *added* to the whole movie experience.

But I didn't want George to get caught.

"Knock it off," I told her.

I put the bucket on the empty seat next to me.

But George had those extra-long monkey arms.

She could reach right around me to scoop out more popcorn.

So I picked up the bucket and reached over George to give it to Keith.

"Eat this, would ya?!" I said to Keith.

"Sure," he said, as he reached for the bucket.

His eyes never left the screen.

Meanwhile, as I passed the popcorn, George plucked out a few more kernels.

Then she pelted the guy in front of us.

The first few times she'd hit him, he didn't mind. But this *last* time was the straw that broke the camel's back.

He turned around. An earring in his eyebrow glittered.

He looked kind of scary.

"If you kids don't knock it off, I'm going to . . ." He stopped midsentence.

He was staring at George.

"Hey, you," he said to George. To *her* he talked

in a high-pitched voice. Like baby talk.

"Are you the little one who broke out of that bad, bad place?" he asked her gently.

She started to screech. Then she stood on her chair and started to hop up and down.

Normally, people would've shushed us. But they were too busy staring.

Staring at the screeching, jumping thing in the movie theater. The thing that wasn't human.

Eyebrow-ring Guy looked from George to me.

"Look. I get what you're doing. It's a good thing. Really. But you need to get her out of here. It's too dangerous."

"Why?" I asked.

I figured he was talking about getting kicked out of the movie theater. You know, for bringing in an animal. (Even though we *did* pay for her ticket. And *did* have the stub to prove it.)

"Because if they find her, they'll take her back. And there won't be anything you can do about it."

"Do about what? And who'll take her back? Do you know George?" I asked.

He shook his head. "I read about her in the newspaper."

The movie was coming to an end. I knew this because everything was blowing up. And people were dying. (I missed it, thanks to Eyebrow-ring Guy, but I'm sure they were the bad guys. That's what was so great about Vin Diesel movies. The bad guys *always* got it in the end.)

Plus, the music was really loud. It was always loudest at the end. You know, to be heard over all the things blowing up.

"Go," Eyebrow-ring Guy said. "Now!"

"Now?!" I choked out. "But we'll miss the end!"

He shook his head. "You're not getting this. If she gets noticed, they'll take her back. And if they take her back, she's in *big* trouble! Her escape brought a lot of focus to their company. All their dirty laundry came out! I'm sure they're not happy. They probably won't let her *live* because of that."

I had no idea what he was talking about. But I didn't like the sound of it. (I really do need to read the paper more often. Or . . . sometimes.)

We needed to get her somewhere. Somewhere safe.

But I had to think where.

"Okay," I said to the guy.

"Good luck," he said back. "Now go."

Keith, George, and I snuck out moments before the credits came on.

"Why did we have to leave so soon?" Keith asked, annoyed.

"Didn't you hear that guy?"

"What guy?" he asked.

"The guy with the earring in his eyebrow."

"No," Keith said. "I was ignoring you. You were making me miss the movie!"

"The *movie*?! You were worried about missing the *movie*?! They're going to kill her if they get her!"

"*Who's* going to kill her?!" Keith yelled.

"Shhh!" I said. "I need to go somewhere and think this out."

We snuck into another theater so I'd have a place to think.

Yes, I felt guilty for . . . you know, cheating the theater. But in all honesty, I'd sunk a ton of money into that place! One free show wasn't going to bankrupt them. Well, that, too, was a lie. *I* hadn't sunk a penny into the place. It was *Keith's* money. But he'd spent enough in that place over the years to build a whole wing! The *Al and Keith* wing! We'd seen the last Vin Diesel movie *six* times! And paid for it each time we'd gone. So I guess I shouldn't feel guilty for this one freebie.

Plus, we *had* paid full price for a monkey! I mean, that should really count for two tickets. Don't you think? George had no *idea* what the movie was about! But she didn't mind sitting there in the dark with us. She was pretty good about the whole thing. (Once the popcorn was gone.)

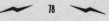

"We've got to go," I told Keith softly.

"Why?" Keith asked.

"It's not safe here. There are too many people. We're taking too big a chance."

Another movie was letting out. I heard a crowd passing by.

So we rushed out and joined the crowd.

"Think anyone noticed George?" I asked Keith.

"You could bring an *alien* to the movies and no one would notice," he said as we walked out.

"Yeah," I said. I kept looking around to make sure no one was watching us.

George was still wearing her red-and-white *Where's Waldo* outfit. With matching hat and sunglasses.

"I'm hungry," Keith said.

"Still have any money?" I asked.

"Not much, but a little," he said. He counted his change.

We slid down a back alley and landed at Mr. Dowd's deli.

Harold Glick worked there.

"I hope Harold doesn't have Sunday off," I said.

Harold was nice. He gave us credit. Then we'd pay him back when we had the money.

CHAPTER

"Hi, Al. Hi, Keith," Mr. Dowd said.

He was a kind man. Short and plump with round, wire-rimmed glasses. But really nice.

The day we were almost gunned down in his deli really made us bond. Now we were like war buddies. Me, Keith, and Mr. Dowd.

Mr. Dowd took a towel from his shoulder and wiped his hands as he came over to us.

"How are my favorite heroes?" he asked.

That's what he always called us. His favorite

heroes. Save the world once, and the man never forgot it. Everyone *else*, on the other hand, forgot pretty quickly.

Anyhow, he was so busy pumping our hands that he hadn't noticed George behind us.

That's sort of how the trouble in his deli started the last time. Except *then* I had a whole terrorist cell behind me. This time I only had a monkey.

The way I figured it was like this: If I could bring a whole band of terrorists to his deli and he didn't hate me, I could probably let him in on our little primate secret.

"Hi, Mr. Dowd. We're looking for a snack," I said.

"Great. What can I get for you?"

I looked at Keith.

Keith shrugged.

"A sandwich?" Mr. Dowd asked.

I looked at Keith again.

Keith shrugged again. Then nodded.

"Sure," I said.

Mr. Dowd walked over to the deli meat counter. "What kind?" Mr. Dowd asked.

"Anything but olive loaf," I said.

Keith laughed. It was a little joke of ours. I guess you had to be there. Plus, it's too long a story to explain.

"How about ham?" Mr. Dowd asked. "Or pastrami?"

I looked at Keith.

"Ham for me, please," Keith said to Mr. Dowd.

"Me too, thanks," I called.

"Special mustard?" Mr. Dowd asked.

"Of course!" Keith and I said together.

Then we laughed. Our laughter made George start screeching. That caught Mr. Dowd's attention.

He looked up and stared at George. Then he tilted his head down. Peered over his glasses for a while. Blinked a couple times. Then looked through his glasses again.

"You know boys, I think I'm going crazy here

but . . . ," Mr. Dowd said. He was still staring at George.

"You're not going crazy, Mr. Dowd," I said.

"Yeah," Keith added. "She's a monkey."

Just then, Harold Glick came out from the back room.

When he almost tripped over George, he sputtered.

He was so startled, he dropped a whole big tray of rice pudding. "What the . . . ," he said as he stared at the monkey.

George ran over to the huge mess and started scooping up handfuls of rice pudding and shoving them to her face.

Keith ran over to George, swiping a spoon from a nearby table. He handed it to her so she'd use it.

"What is your problem?" I yelled at Keith.

"Hey! That's the only outfit she has! I don't want her to get it dirty," he said defensively.

Harold Glick stared at Keith. "There's a *chimp*

in the deli. Eating rice pudding off the *floor*. And you're worried about its *outfit*?"

"It was expensive," Keith answered.

"No, it wasn't!" I said. "It was half off! At the thrift store," I explained to the stunned Mr. Dowd and Harold Glick.

We all watched as George stuffed herself with rice pudding. Using a spoon.

"Not that that doesn't explain everything, boys," Mr. Dowd said patiently. "But what are you doing with a monkey?"

"We found her," Keith said.

"At the park," I added.

Harold was still staring at George. "She's not a monkey. She's a chimp," he said.

"There's a difference?" I asked.

"Yes," Harold said. He was still staring.

I shrugged. "Whatever."

"Guys?" Harold asked Keith and me. "Do you think maybe *she's* the chimp that's been splashed all over the news?"

That must be what the guy at the movies was talking about.

I looked at Keith. He shrugged.

"I don't know. What's *that* about?" I asked Harold.

"The news? Last night?" he said.

I shook my head. "I spent all night watching *Teletubbies* and *Barney*. Oh, and the *Big Comfy Couch*."

Harold looked totally disgusted.

"Not for me, Harold! For George!"

We all looked at George. She was still sucking up rice pudding. Once again, my mind flew to monkey diarrhea. I hoped she had an iron stomach.

"How about today's newspaper?" Harold said.

I'm not big on reading the newspaper. Only the comics. You'd think I'd learned my lesson after the whole "Princess Beth" thing. But that's another story.

"The Sunday paper?" Harold asked. He looked between Keith and me.

"We took George to the zoo and then the movies," Keith said. Then he started cracking up and I knew he was thinking about his joke.

Maybe I was a little tired. Or possibly delirious. Because all of a sudden I thought it was really funny, too. Keith and I were cracking up. Meanwhile, Mr. Dowd and Harold stared between the rice-pudding-eating chimp and us.

Harold walked to a table and sifted through sections of the Sunday *Times*. He must've found what he was looking for, because he walked over to Keith and I and snapped the paper to its full length.

There, on the front cover, was a picture of a monkey. Or a chimp.

We looked from the picture to George. Then back to the picture. Then back at George.

"Nope. It's not her," Keith said with finality.

It did sort of look a *little* like her. But what did I know about chimp facial features?

Harold shook the newspaper. "Look again," he said through clenched teeth.

Across the top of the page were the words: MISSING CHIMPANZEE!

"It's not her," Keith repeated.

"Then who is that?" Harold asked. He was pointing to George.

"A different chimp," Keith said.

"So you think there are *two* missing chimps?" Mr. Dowd asked Keith.

I looked at Keith.

"For all I know, there are millions of missing chimps in this world," he said.

He did have a point.

"But in this *town*?" Harold asked Keith.

"How am *I* supposed to know?" Keith barked back. "What do I look like? Some kind of missing chimp expert?"

I was growing tired of this chat. "Let's read the paper and see," I said.

Harold handed me the paper.

"What's it say?" Keith asked.

"From what I can tell," I started, "there's a missing chimp."

Harold slapped his forehead and rolled his

eyes. "Oh, for God's sake! Give me that!"

He took the paper back. He looked at the article.

"A company called Bosting Industries is missing one of its test monkeys," he said.

"What kind of company?" Keith asked.

Harold looked at the paper again. "A company that makes makeup."

"Well, that's stupid!" I said.

"Why?" Harold asked. He looked like he really didn't want to know my answer.

"Because who puts makeup on a *monkey*?" I said.

"See?" Keith said. "It's not her."

We all looked at George.

She was still going at the pudding full force. Almost had it all cleaned up, too!

"They don't *apply* it to the chimps! They *test* it on chimps!" Harold said.

"Like how?" I asked.

Harold buried his head back into the article.

"Oh, my God," he said. "That's awful!"

"What's awful?" Mr. Dowd, Keith, and I asked at the same time.

"It says here they drip the makeup in her eyes to see if it will irritate them," he said quietly.

CHAPTER
10

We were all looking at George.

She finished the entire tray of rice pudding. She looked back at us and burped. Loud and proud.

"Did they hurt you, girl? Huh?" I asked her.

"Yeah. Did they hurt you, George?" Keith asked.

"You sound like a Lassie movie," Mr. Dowd said.

"What's a Lassie movie?" Keith asked.

Mr. Dowd laughed. It was a hollow sound. Not like he was really laughing. "They're these old movies."

"Doesn't a kid always fall down a well in them?" Harold asked Mr. Dowd.

"Yes." Mr. Dowd laughed again. Only this time, it sounded like a real laugh. "Then Lassie—a collie dog—always knows where the child is."

"How do they know the dog knows?" Keith asked.

"Because they ask the dog," Mr. Dowd explained.

"And it speaks to them?" Keith asked. He looked totally amazed.

I rolled my eyes. This was a really stupid conversation. But I think we were all avoiding the one we should *really* be having.

"Lassie usually barks," Mr. Dowd tried to explain.

"And people understand what she's saying?" Keith asked.

This little chat couldn't get more stupid if anyone tried.

Mr. Dowd must've felt the same way. He shrugged and said, "They usually figured it out."

Once that sparkling discussion was over, everyone was quiet.

Out of the corner of my eye, I saw an old couple walking toward the deli.

"Quick, Mr. Dowd. Someone's coming," I said.

He ran to the front door and locked it. Then he turned the sign from OPEN to CLOSED.

Well, on *our* side it went from CLOSED to OPEN. But on the outside, it must've gone from OPEN to CLOSED.

The older man tried the door and then saw the sign. He and his wife then kept walking down the street.

"Oh, my God. I'm harboring a . . . a . . . ," Mr. Dowd got stuck on the next word.

"What *is* she?" Keith asked.

"She's not a convict," Harold said.

"Or an escaped prisoner," I added.

"She's more like a victim," Mr. Dowd said.

We were all staring at George.

George walked up to Mr. Dowd.

He looked scared.

"Don't worry, Mr. Dowd. She won't hurt you," I said.

She jumped on Mr. Dowd and tried to take his glasses.

"Oh. We forgot to tell you. She has a thing for glasses," Keith said.

"Is it any wonder?" Harold asked.

"What do you mean?" I said.

"If these people hurt her eyes on a regular basis, she probably sees glasses as eye guards. They are a way to protect her eyes," he explained.

"Wow," I said. "You're right."

"We can't let them take her back there!" Keith wailed.

"No," I agreed. "We can't!"

"Then aren't we, ah . . . ," Mr. Dowd shook his head.

"What's the matter?" I asked him.

"I'm trying to think of a word for what we're doing. But I can't."

"Kidnapping?" Harold asked.

"No," I said. "That can't be the word."

"Chimp-napping?" Keith asked.

"I don't think that's a word," I said.

"How about: Grand Theft Ape?" Keith suggested.

"Grand Theft Ape?" I repeated with a roll of my eyes.

"Yeah," Keith said proudly. "Like 'Grand Theft Auto.' Only with a monkey."

"Then it would be Grand Theft Monkey, you imbecile!" I said to Keith. "Monkeys aren't apes, Keith! *Everyone* knows that!"

"Yeah," Keith admitted. "But it doesn't flow as well as Grand Theft Ape."

"Has anyone ever told you that you're an idiot?" I asked him.

"Besides you?"

"Yeah. Besides me," I said.

"Yes."

Mr. Dowd cleared his throat loudly. "Um, boys? I think we need to focus here."

The church down the street just let out. And there was a whole *bunch* of people heading our way.

"Look, boys. I've got to take in these customers," Mr. Dowd said nervously.

"Can Al and Keith take her into the back room?" Harold asked.

Mr. Dowd let out a huge sigh. "Great idea!"

"There's a back room?" I asked.

"Yes, it's my office," Mr. Dowd said.

"I'll take you there," Harold said.

"Have any bananas?" Keith asked before leaving.

We all looked at George.

"Don't you think she's full?" Harold asked.

"She just ate enough rice pudding for eighty people!" Mr. Dowd said.

"They're for me." Keith shrugged.

I pelted him on the shoulder.

"What?!" he said. "I had a craving!"

"Shut up. Would you?" I said to my best friend the nitwit.

"I'll have Harold bring you those sandwiches," Mr. Dowd said. "And some sodas."

"Sounds great!" I said honestly.

"Just stay back there. Okay, boys?" he said as he unlocked the front door.

"Sure thing," I said.

The office was cramped, but I noticed a computer.

Harold came back in with the sandwiches.

"Hey, can you fire this thing up for me?" I asked him.

It was an old machine, but it worked.

"Does it have Internet access?" I asked Harold.

"Yes. But it's dial-up, so it's slow," he said.

"It's not like we're going anywhere for a while," I said.

Harold had to get back out there to help with the customers.

As we waited for my Google search page to load, I asked Keith a question.

"Remember when you told me your mother's allergic to monkeys?"

"Yeah," he said.

"Well, there's got to be more to that story," I said.

"Like what?" Keith asked.

George was sitting on Keith's lap, trading glasses with him. Now that we knew *why* she always did that, we let her. We felt sorry for her.

"Like, how did your mom find out she was allergic to monkeys?"

"She was tested."

"They test for allergies to monkeys? That's part of a routine physical?" I asked.

I mean, it sounded stupid to me. But what did *I* know?

"No, silly! Her ear looked like broccoli!"

Oh, yeah. That explained a lot.

I stared at Keith.

He stared back at me.

George stared at both of us.

"Is there *more* to that story?" I was losing patience.

Keith shrugged. "I was little. We were at the zoo. She touched a monkey."

I waited for more. Nothing.

"And?" I screamed.

"And she had an itch on her ear."

The sad thing was, I got the link. I must've been Keith's friend for too long.

"So she scratched her ear," I said.

"Yeah," Keith nodded.

"And it blew up like a broccoli," I finished.

He looked at me like *I* was an idiot. "Well, yeah. What did you *think* happened?"

My hands balled into fists.

There were times I really wanted to deck him. This was one of those times.

If it weren't for George sitting in his lap, I would have.

But weirdly, she cleared her throat just then.

It was like she was saying, "Um, excuse me. Are you two done? Because I'd like to know what you're going to do with me."

All that in one little throat clearing. George was one smart chimp. Let me tell you!

CHAPTER

11

My Google page had loaded.

I was sorting through all the websites that fit my search words.

I finally found what I was looking for.

"Hey look, Keith," I said as I pointed to the monitor.

"What?"

"It's a place that saves animals," I said.

I tried to see where it was. I had to go to their "contact us" page.

"Are they in town?" Keith asked.

I shook my head. "No. But they're close."

"Maybe they'll know what to do," Keith said.

"I'm hoping," I said as I scrolled down to find their phone number.

"Call them," Keith said.

The area code was different than ours. "I'd better ask Mr. Dowd if it's okay. It's long distance," I said.

"I'll wait here with George. You go ask," Keith said.

I was almost out the door when Keith said, "And see if you can get some chips."

I nodded, closing the door behind me.

When Mr. Dowd saw me, he got nervous. He looked around.

"Don't worry. She's still in your office," I said.

"Good," he said.

"Can I use your phone to call a place?" I asked.

"To where?" he asked.

"The Animal Protective Agency. In Dunsberry."

"You mean the Animal Protection League?" he asked.

I shrugged. "Yeah. I think so."

"Hm. I didn't know they were in Dunsberry. But yes, sure, Al. They're a good organization. Go ahead."

"And can Keith and I have some chips?" I asked.

"Sure, son. Take whatever you'd like."

He was serving up some chocolate pudding. He added some canned whipped cream on top. You know the kind. The kind that squirts out of the little plastic tip.

Once, when I was little, my parents went out and I had a babysitter. I snuck out of my room to see what she was doing. She was eating canned whipped cream. Right out of the can!

It looked like fun.

My mom would *never* let me do that! Once she found me drinking right out of the milk carton and had a cow!

So the next day, when my mom was in the bathroom, I tried it. I filled my mouth with fluffy whipped cream!

And you know what? It *was* fun!

I figured if George got a kick out of Milk Duds, she'd *really* like canned whipped cream.

I mean, she ate enough rice pudding to go with it! Didn't she?

So I took the can back in with me too.

Hey, he *had* said, "take whatever you'd like." Right?

"Cool," Keith said as I came back. "Chips *and* whipped cream!"

"That's for George," I said.

I showed her how to shake the can. Then I aimed it at my mouth. Then I squirted some in.

George didn't look impressed.

So I took her hand and squirted some on her hand.

She looked grossed out and almost wiped it on her outfit.

Keith panicked. "Quick, get a napkin!" he shouted. He grabbed George's hand.

He was really freaking out about that outfit! Weird. But I got a paper towel and wiped it off. I didn't want to have to hear him if she *did* ruin her outfit.

"Show her," Keith said.

I squirted some into my hand and then ate it.

George watched intently.

I did it again.

Then Keith did it.

Then I squirted some in her hand again.

This time she ate it. And she *loved* it!

I offered her the can and she took it right away. I put my hand on top of hers and bent the nozzle. To show her how to make the stuff come out.

She was psyched!

"Go ahead," I told her.

She screeched with joy.

I figured she'd squirt some in her other hand. But no. Instead, she put the can up to her mouth.

I could tell she liked the feel of it filling her mouth.

The only problem was, she didn't know when to stop. And before I could stop her, she had a face full of whipped cream.

That's when Harold came in to see how things were going.

"What are you *doing* to her?" he shouted. He wiped her face off carefully.

"Hey," I said. "She did it to herself."

Harold took the can from George.

She snatched it back, stuck it into her mouth, and fizzed out a perfect load!

"See?" I said to Harold. "You just caught her on her first try. She learns really fast!"

"Too bad I can't say the same for you two," he muttered.

We stuck our tongues out at Harold.

George thought that was hilarious. So she stuck hers out at Harold too.

And gave him a raspberry.

Little bits of whipped cream splattered everywhere!

"Only you two could turn a chimp into an idiot in under five minutes!" Harold said with a big sigh. "Now clean that up, would you?"

"Don't get so huffy about it!" I said to Harold.

"Hey, you didn't have to clean up the rice pudding puddle!" he said back.

"Well, *you're* the one who dropped it!" I said.

He shook his head. "Because I wasn't expecting to see a *chimp* in the middle of the *deli*!" he sputtered.

I tried to enlighten him. "You really should be more prepared for the unexpected."

Harold stared at me, then rolled his eyes. "Yeah, especially when *you two* are around!"

Mr. Dowd opened the door and shoved his hefty body into the small, crowded room. "Have you reached them yet?"

"I haven't called," I said. "I'll call now."

I dialed the number on the monitor.

"Hello. Animal Protective Agency."

"Hi. My name is Al . . . ," I started.

Keith punched me in the chest, knocking the air out of me.

"No names!" he said in a stage whisper.

"Oh. Yeah. Right," I said to him.

"Hello?" the lady on the phone said. "Anyone there?"

"Sorry," I said. "Um, hi."

"Hi," she said.

"You know anything about that missing chimp?" I asked her.

"Who wants to know?" she said snappishly.

I didn't know what to say to that. "We think we found her," I blurted out.

"Oh, my goodness. Thank God!" she said with excitement. "Is she safe?"

I looked at George. I thought she was smiling. But I couldn't tell. Her face was covered with whipped cream. "She seems to be."

"Oh, what a mess *that* was," the woman started.

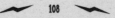

"We were in the building. Trying to rescue the animals. And we only got a couple animals out of there when security came in!"

Wow. What a story!

"Of course they took back the animals we freed. But no one could find that one chimp," she said.

"Well, we found her. Or, should I say, she found us."

I thought I heard the woman clapping her hands. "How delightful! So one did get free!" she trilled.

"Seems that way," I said.

"You can't take her back there. They use the animals for testing. They *hurt* the animals! It's barbaric—*horrible*!" she said. She was really upset. I could tell.

"That's why I'm calling you," I said. "I don't want to take her back there. But I can't keep her. I don't even know what to feed her!"

"What have you given her so far?" the woman asked.

"Mayonnaise, Milk Duds, rice pudding, and whipped cream," I said. "She hated bologna."

The woman was speechless. "Where are you?" she finally asked.

"At a deli," I said.

"You're at a deli," she repeated. "And all you could come up with to feed her is mayo, Milk Duds, and rice pudding?"

"Well, the mayo was from my home. She had the Milk Duds at the movies. It was only when we hit the deli that she had the rice pudding and the whipped cream."

The woman was once again speechless.

"Miss?" I asked.

"Yes?" she said.

"Is something wrong?" I asked.

She was quiet for a moment before she said, "No. I'm just amazed, that's all."

"Amazed? At what?" I asked.

"The fact that a *chimp* had a better time while *lost*, than I've *ever* had on a *date*!"

"Sorry to hear that," I said honestly.

I heard her snort through her nose. "Yes, well . . ."

"So now what happens?" I asked.

"Can I come and get her?" she asked.

I had to think about that. "Well, that depends."

"On what?"

"On what you're going to do with her," I said. "She didn't seem too thrilled about the zoo."

"You took her to the zoo, *too*?" she asked. She sounded like she didn't believe this conversation.

"Yeah. To see if she knew anyone. Or looked like she missed home or something," I said.

"And did she know anyone or miss it?" she asked.

"Nah. She didn't seem to. But she liked the elephants," I said.

No answer.

"Miss?"

Nothing.

"*Miss?*"

Still nothing.

Finally I heard her say, "I have *got* to find myself a better type of guy. I can*not* believe a chimp was shown a *better* time while on shore leave than I've *ever* had. *Ever!*"

This lady sure did have some issues.

"Maybe you're just attracted to the wrong type of guy," I said gently.

"Yeah, that's what my mother keeps telling me."

I waited to see if she'd get back to business.

When the long pause turned longer, I spoke. "Look. You think you could pick up George soon? My friend Keith's mom is allergic and I've hidden her from my mom for two days now. But tomorrow's school and we won't be able to keep her."

"I'll come out there right away. It's Sunday and everyone else is home . . . with *someone*. So I'll come alone. As always."

CHAPTER

12

I told the lady where we were and hung up. "So what did she say?" Keith asked.

"She can't find a good guy to date. She's always alone on weekends. Oh, and her mother nags her a lot."

"About the *chimp*!" Harold said forcefully.

"Oh. She'll come right over."

"Good," Mr. Dowd said. He saw the can of whipped cream sitting on the desk. "I've been looking all over for this," he said as he reached for the can.

George was faster.

She swiped it right out of his reach. Then she tipped it to her mouth and gave herself a good squirt.

"On second thought," Mr. Dowd said, "keep it. I'll get a new can."

George blew monkey kisses at him.

"She's saying thank you," Keith said to Mr. Dowd.

"Tell her she's welcome," Mr. Dowd said back.

"You just did," I said. "She's very smart, you know."

We all heard the bell on the counter ring.

"I've got to get back out there," Mr. Dowd said.

"We'll stay here, waiting," I said.

About fifty minutes and two cans of whipped cream later, Mr. Dowd showed a young woman into the room.

"That was fast," I said.

"I raced over. I'm so excited that she escaped."

The lady looked at George and smiled widely.

"I'm Vicky," she said as she held out her hand to me. "From the Animal Protective Agency."

"I figured," I said. "I'm, um . . ." I looked at Keith to see if he thought it was okay to give out names now.

"What? You can't remember your own name?" Keith asked me.

"No, you moron! I was looking at you to see if it was okay to give out names now," I said.

"Oh, I won't do anything with your names," Vicky said. "And I certainly won't do anything to get *you* in trouble! We're on the same side here."

"The Animal Protection League is a wonderful group," Mr. Dowd said in his usual jolly way.

"Oh. I'm not with the Animal Protection League. Well, not anymore. I *used* to be. But I left."

I looked to Mr. Dowd to straighten this out. I was confused.

"What do you mean you 'used' to work for them?" Mr. Dowd asked the lady.

"It's always been my dream to save animals. To

protect them. But that place had too much paper-work. Too much red tape."

"Why didn't you just use the clear tape?" I asked her.

"Yeah," Keith agreed.

"She's not talking about real tape," Mr. Dowd said.

"Then what kind of tape *is* it?" I asked.

"It's not tape at *all*!" she said loudly.

I looked at Keith. He looked at me. We shrugged.

"It means they have rules. Lots of rules," she said, a little calmer.

"So?" I asked.

"Things took too long," she said. "The whole time I was pushing papers, animals were getting hurt. Each minute, each hour, each day I wasn't saving animals, they weren't being saved!"

She sure was charged about her cause!

"If I were still with the Animal Protection League, I'd have to give her back to Bosting. Then I'd have to get evidence to prove the abuse. Lots of paperwork. And then we'd need a warrant to get her out of there." She was pointing to George. "It could take months."

"Well, *that* doesn't seem right!" Keith said.

She looked angry and upset. "I just couldn't do it anymore. Change happened too slowly!"

"So what group *are* you with?" Mr. Dowd asked her.

"The Animal Protective Agency," she said.

"It sounds official," Keith said.

"Yes. We wanted it that way," she said.

"But it's not?" I asked.

"Um, not really. Let's just say we're not really bound by many restraints."

I was trying to understand all of this. "So you're, like, rogue animal rescuers," I said.

She smiled with pride. "I like that!"

She stuck out her hand. "I didn't catch your name."

"Al Netti," I said as I shook her hand. "And that's Keith."

"Hi," Keith said with a big smile.

Vicky waved at Keith. "And you must be our little escape artist," she said to George.

"That's George," I said.

Vicky looked confused. "The missing chimp is a female."

I rolled my eyes. "Keith named her."

"Oh," Vicky said primly.

Vicky and George played together for a little while.

"So we don't have to bring her back, right?" I asked.

"*I'm* not bringing her back!" Vicky said.

"What about the other animals at that place?" Keith asked her.

She shrugged and frowned.

"Can't we get them out too?" I asked her.

She looked at us. Measuring us up. "I couldn't do that with you. It's too dangerous. And you're . . . kids."

That made us laugh. "If you *knew* some of the

things we've been through, you wouldn't say that! We've fought off terrorists," I said.

"And people who were trying to overthrow a country's monarchy," Keith added.

"And mean psychos who were trying to steal the designs for a suitcase bomb," I finished.

Vicky looked at Mr. Dowd.

He smiled and nodded. "I know. It's hard to believe. But it's true."

She looked back at us.

"Let us help you," I said.

"Let *us* save those animals!" Keith added.

"You know," she said slowly. "I *am* all the way over here. And *do* have the van."

"And it's a Sunday," I noted. "So who'll be there working?"

"Nobody," Keith said with a wicked smile.

"What do you say we go free some victims?" I asked her.

She shook her head. "I don't know about this," she said.

"I do!" I said.

"It's illegal," she said.

"What they do to those animals should be illegal!" I countered.

"Yeah. Why *are* they allowed to do it?" Keith asked.

It was a good question. "I thought animal testing wasn't allowed anymore."

Vicky nodded. "For large corporations, it's not. But Bosting's a little company. So they don't have the same government laws and standards."

"Well, *that* doesn't seem right!" I said.

"The laws are changing, so it'll apply to them someday. Hopefully soon," she said.

I looked at George. "But not soon enough!" I argued.

She nodded. "That's the way I feel. It's why I left the League. Things changed too slowly."

"Okay," I said. "We *have* to do this! Take us to Bosting Industries."

"Yeah," Keith said. He held up his fist and pounded the air. "Let's free *everyone*!"

Mr. Dowd sighed deeply. "I didn't hear any of this," he said.

I nodded. "Thanks, Mr. Dowd. For everything."

"No problem, Al. Stop in again. Anytime," he said. "It's always so . . . exciting."

We all laughed.

When we got outside, the "van" turned out to be a huge truck. I'd wondered how the three of us would fit in a van and have room for a bunch of animals. But I didn't have to worry.

"After we get the animals—*if* we get the animals— I'll drop you guys off at your homes," Vicky said.

"What about the animals?" I asked.

"I'll take them with me. I know people who can help them. You won't have to worry," she said sweetly.

I felt like Vin Diesel. Going off to a place filled with bad guys. Saving the little guy.

It felt great!

I could feel the blood pumping through my veins.

"This is cool!" I said to Vicky and Keith.

"Yeah," Keith said.

"I have the plans behind the seat. If you want to take a look," Vicky said.

"What plans?" I asked.

"Plans. Of Bosting Industries. You know, the layout of the building."

As cool as that sounded, I really didn't know how to read them. So why waste the time or energy?

"That's okay. We'll follow your lead," I said to Vicky.

When we got there, it was really dark.

The building was empty. It sat in an industrial park that was totally deserted.

"This is going to be a piece of cake!" I said in my best Vin Diesel imitation.

"So how do we get in?" Keith asked.

"Last time we went in through a pipe, down by the stream," Vicky said.

I got a little worried. "Is it a big pipe or a little pipe?" I asked.

"Oh, don't worry. You'll fit," Vicky said.

"He gets a little freaked out in tight places," Keith said.

"Hm," Vicky said. "How freaked out?"

"Like Kramer, when he sees clowns."

"Kramer?" Vicky asked.

"Yeah. From *Seinfeld*."

Vicky laughed. "That's funny."

"Not for *me*," I said.

"Maybe it's more like Indiana Jones, when he sees snakes," Keith said.

Vicky rolled her eyes. "And I had to be an English lit major!" she muttered to herself.

"What's that?" I asked.

I had no clue what she was talking about.

"I majored in English literature," she said.

I shrugged. "Still nothing," I explained.

"The classics," she said. "I studied the classics."

"You mean books?" I asked.

She stared at me. "Yes. Books."

"How are you with *A Tale of Two Cities*?"

She laughed. "That was my specialty."

"I mean, what does it all mean, anyhow? 'It was the best of times. It was the worst of times.' Wouldn't they cancel each other out?" I asked.

"Yeah, making it just an 'okay' time?" Keith asked.

Vicky laughed. Then looked at us. "Oh. You're serious."

We shrugged.

"It's not like that at all," Vicky said. "You're looking at things from the wrong angle."

"Well, would you mind explaining it to Keith? If he doesn't have it down by tomorrow, he'll fail English."

"Sure," she said. "No problem."

She spent the next half hour explaining the whole book to Keith.

"You know, when you explain it, it sounds kind of cool," Keith said truthfully.

"Yeah, it's a pretty cool book," Vicky said.

Keith laughed. "Not when I read it. I had no idea what it was about."

"You have to learn from a good teacher," Vicky said.

"Mrs. White's tough," I told her.

But Vicky shrugged. "Tough doesn't mean good. A good teacher explains everything. Makes the hard stuff seem easy."

"Yeah," Keith said. "I guess."

"Look, we'd better get this rescue mission started," Vicky said.

I turned to the back of the van. "You stay here, George. Okay? We'll be right back with your friends."

CHAPTER
13

We were at the pipe.

"Okay. So you're afraid of tight spaces," Vicky said to me.

"Yeah," I said.

"And you," she said to Keith. "You're probably too big to fit."

He looked insulted.

"How about if I go in alone? Through here," she said.

What were we going to do? Argue?

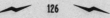

"Wait by the side entrance," she said, pointing. "I'll come get you as soon as I'm in."

Then she was gone.

Keith and I walked to the side entrance.

"Well, this is fun," I said.

Keith nodded. "Yeah. And now I know what that stupid book's about."

"I'd have to say this was a good day," I added.

Keith agreed. "First the zoo. Then a Vin Diesel movie. Then the deli. And now this."

"Yeah, It's like *Mission Impossible*," I said.

"Except . . . it *is* possible," Keith said. "So it's more like . . . Mission *Possible*."

I was about to tell him he was an idiot when Vicky came to the door.

"Come on in, guys," she said with a wide grin.

We followed her to the area with the animals.

"This is one testing lab," she said. "There's another on the other side of the building."

We nodded.

"You get the animals from this one," she said. "Since we're already here."

"Sounds good," Keith said.

I felt great. Just like Vin Diesel. I was ready to free some innocent victims. "Let's move it, team!" I said to Keith.

"Don't you want to know what to do?" Vicky asked.

Oh. Yeah. That would help.

"So what do we do?" I asked.

"Start with the most docile animals," she said.

"Docile?" I asked.

She nodded. "It means . . . calm, gentle, tame."

Keith started to freak. "You mean there's untamed animals here?"

I knew he was thinking lions. And tigers. And bears.

"No, no, no," Vicky said. "They're all pretty much tame. Just some are easier to handle and corral, that's all."

"Like?" I asked.

"Like the chimps. They're a good place to start. Then move on to the rats."

Keith made a face. "The *rats*?"

"They're safe and clean. Like mice. Don't worry," she told him.

He didn't look convinced.

"I'll handle the rats," I told Keith.

Keith let out a sigh and smiled. "Thanks."

"Just save the rabbits for last," Vicky instructed.

"Why?" I asked. I figured they'd be pretty, um, what was the word? Oh, yeah. Docile.

"They hop all over the place," she said. "They're the hardest to corral."

I pictured a cowboy with a lasso, trying to corral a herd of rabbits. The rabbits were hopping all over the place. It was a madhouse! Total chaos. And the cowboys couldn't get their lassos around the fuzzy little guys. It was funny. I started to laugh at the silly pictures in my head.

Vicky looked at me like I was nuts. "I'll be at the other lab."

"Good luck," I called to her back.

"You too," she called back to me.

Why is it that things seem so easy until they get hard?

Everything was going great.

We had the chimps free. The birds, too. The mice and rats were out and running around also.

Of course that meant Keith was standing on a table.

He was shaking and trying not to scream. Really not much of a help to me. At all!

I'd done what Vicky said. I saved the rabbits for last.

I had about three more cages of rabbits to unhook. Then, suddenly, the lights went on.

My right hand was on one lock. My left on another.

That would leave only one rabbit cage.

A deep voice said, "Don't."

I froze.

"You talking to me?" I asked.

I turned slowly, lifting the two latches in my hands.

Two more frec. One to go.

Would I do it?

Could I?

I slowly slid over to the last rabbit cage.

"I said *halt*," the deep voice said.

I turned to face him. My hand flicked open the last cage. "No, you didn't. You said 'don't.' Not 'halt,'" I told him.

"A wise guy, are ya?" he asked.

The last rabbit jumped to the ground.

The sudden movement made the deep-voiced man draw his gun.

Keith screamed.

"Security detail," the man said.

I stared at the man. "Wow. What are the odds of that?" I asked him.

"Of what?" he asked.

"Of your parents naming you Security? And your last name being Detail?"

The guy shook his head. "I wasn't *introducing* myself! I was stating my credentials." He flashed his badge.

"So you're sort of like a rent-a-cop?" I asked.

A vein bulged in his head.

I got the impression that he hated it when people said that.

"I'm a *security* guard! That's a valid *job*, you know!" His gun was flailing all about.

"Hey. Chill out, dude," I said. I was watching his gun.

The guy looked really ticked off. "I'm not a *dude*!"

Keith stopped screaming. "You're a *lady*?"

We stared at him. He didn't *look* like a lady.

The guy was furious. "I'm an officer of the *law*!" he shouted. His arms were waving about and his gun went off.

All heck broke loose!

Birds were squawking. Rabbits hopping. Chimps screeching. Rats and mice were running every which way.

It was bedlam!

The security guard looked like he was going to have a heart attack.

That vein in his head looked like it was going to burst.

"It's all right," I said to the guard. "It's not your fault."

Keith made a face at me. "Yes, it is!"

The guard now had his gun trained on me.

I looked at Keith. "Would you *please* shut up? I was trying to calm him down!"

"I'll catch you *this* time," the guard said to me.

"What?" I asked him. He seemed to be in a fog or something.

"I have to catch you," he repeated.

"Why?" I asked.

"You're the same ones who came and destroyed the lab last time."

I thought of Vicky. I figured if I could keep this guy here, she was safe.

The animals were trashing the place. The

chimps were pulling the cages off the tables. The birds were picking up stuff with their beaks and throwing it all around. The rabbits were dragging the clutter all over the place. And the rats and mice were burrowing through the mess like gophers.

"Well," I said. "It would appear that the *animals* were the ones that trashed the place. Not us," I added.

That *really* ticked the guy off!

I could tell he was thinking about what to do with us.

"Okay. You," he said to me. He was pointing his gun at me. "Get up there with the screaming kid."

He was waving his gun between Keith and me.

Before another shot went off by mistake, I climbed on the table with Keith.

We stood there, staring down at him.

"Now what?" I asked.

Wow, was *that* the wrong question to ask. He was on the edge as it was. It seemed my question pushed him over the edge.

"Yes. I need to do more," he said to himself like he was insane. "But what?"

He looked at us.

"Don't ask *me*," I said. "I'm the one who asked *you*."

The guy growled with anger and his gun went off again. This time he missed a bird by a hair. Or a feather.

There was more squawking, hopping, screeching, and running. Only louder. And faster.

"Take off your clothes!" the guy finally said.

"Excuse me?" I asked.

"You heard me," he said. "Take off your clothes. In all this chaos, I don't want you to escape."

"And . . . taking off our clothes would stop us, how?" I asked him.

His eyes closed to wary slits. "No one likes being seen in their underwear."

Hmm. He had a point.

CHAPTER
14

We all stood there. But nobody moved.

"Get moving!" the guy roared. To make his point, he fired his gun again. This time, he hit a window. Glass shattered everywhere.

"I'm shy," I said. "I don't disrobe for just *anyone!*" I said.

"You're not *wearing* a robe," Keith whispered to me.

I rolled my eyes. "It means undress, you nimrod!"

"Oh," Keith said to me. "Then what he said goes for me, too," he said to the edgy guard.

We seemed to have pushed his buttons. He was *really* mad now. "I'll kill you *both!*" he roared.

I started to strip. "No need. No need. We're getting undressed. See?"

"I *knew* I should've worn more layers," Keith said to himself.

We each stripped down to our underwear. Anything further would be, you know, gross.

"Hey," Keith said as he looked at me. "Look at *you.*"

"What about me?" I asked slowly.

I looked at the guard. His gun was still aimed right at us.

"You're wearing boxers!" Keith said.

I didn't like the way Keith was looking at me. "So?" I asked.

"I thought you were a 'briefs' guy," Keith said.

"I was."

"So why did you change?" he asked.

"I don't know." I shrugged. "Just thought I'd try these out. Plus, my mom bought 'em and stuck 'em in my drawer."

There was a long, quiet pause.

"They look good," Keith said.

It kind of freaked me out, so I didn't say anything.

"You look good in red plaid," Keith blurted out.

Okay. That was enough. "Would you please shut up?" I said loudly.

"Why? I was just trying to be nice," he said.

"Just shut up, Keith. Okay?"

He looked hurt.

"Look," I said. "I'm sorry. I'm just not in the mood for this."

Keith nodded. "For what? Getting caught? Being forced to undress at gunpoint?"

"No, you moron! I'm not in the mood for talking about my *underwear*!"

Keith stared blankly at me. "So you *were* in the mood for the *other* stuff?"

"No!" I shouted. "I *had* to go through that! But I don't *have* to discuss my choice of *underwear!*"

"I was just trying to cheer things up," Keith said with a big frown.

I rolled my eyes. *Please, God, don't let me kill him now. I really want to, but don't let me kill him now. Okay?*

"Thank you, Keith. I'm cheered up. Really. All cheered up. Your comment that I look good in my red boxers? It made all the difference."

"I'm so glad," Keith said with a huge smile.

"Yes, Keith. Now I feel all better. Like I have no problems. None. The world is my coaster."

"Your what?" Keith asked.

"My coaster."

"What does *that* mean?" he asked.

"I don't know. I heard it on an old movie. The guy was all happy. Everything had worked out okay for him. I *thought* he said 'the world is my *oyster*' but my mother was blowing her nose real loudly when he'd said it."

"Was she sick?" Keith asked.

"No, it was just a sad movie that turned out happy. She always cries at movies like that. Anyhow, it didn't make sense to me."

"Yeah, I don't get it either," Keith agreed.

"So I figured he must have said 'coaster.' You know, instead of 'oyster'."

Keith nodded. "The world is my coaster," he said aloud. Then he nodded again.

"I figured he meant that he could put his glass down anywhere on it. You know, the world is his coaster."

Keith looked impressed. "Makes sense to me."

I nodded.

"You're really smart, Al," Keith said with feeling. "I don't care *what* the teachers say about you."

"I know," I agreed.

"If they knew you like I know you, they'd be amazed," he said.

I knew what he meant. Sometimes, when one of my teachers asked me a question, I'd give them a *great* answer! One that just popped into my head! Out of nowhere! Then they'd usually shake their head, wipe their hand over their face, and say, "Al, you're amazing."

"Would you two please . . . shut . . . *up*?" the guard asked. "I can't *take* any more!" he screamed.

"What's *his* problem?" Keith asked me quietly.

I shrugged. "I don't know. He's a little tightly wound."

"That's why they kicked me out of the police academy," he said to us sadly.

I felt kind of sorry for him. "Maybe you can work on that. You know, learn how to chill out a little. And then go back and try at the academy again."

"You think?" he asked me.

I put my hands on my hips and tried to look in control. Well at least as "in control" as a person standing on a table in just his socks and boxers *could* look. "Sure," I said to him. "I don't see why not."

"My parents were really disappointed," he said.

"Because I got kicked out of the academy," he explained.

"You were younger then. Less experienced," I said.

"That's true," he agreed.

"Well now you're older and wiser. I'll bet you could do it this time," I said smoothly.

"You think so?" he asked hopefully.

Not! "Sure!"

Just then I heard the sounds of sirens wailing in the distance. "Um. What was your name again?" I asked the guard.

"Stanley. Stanley Svenson."

"Nice to meet you," I said.

"Likewise," he answered.

"So, um, Stanley?"

"Yes?"

"By any chance, are you an animal lover?"

"Why, yes I am, Al."

"Well, this place you work at—Bosting Industries. You know they hurt these animals. Right?"

He looked uncomfortable. "I try not to think about it."

Vicky must've been listening at the doorway. "You try not to *think* about it?" she hollered as she burst into the room.

Keith and I tried to cover ourselves. But hands can only cover so much, you know.

We needn't have bothered. She was too busy throwing dagger eyes at Stanley to even notice we were in the room.

"They torture these poor animals. And for what? Makeup? I don't even like animal testing for things that are important! But for *makeup*?"

Stanley was staring at Vicky. Not shocked staring. Or "where did *you* come from" staring. But goo-goo-eyed staring.

Great.

"So what should we do about it?" Stanley asked her.

The sirens were still far away, but were getting closer.

"Look. Just let us take them out of here. Let us take them where they belong," she said.

Stanley thought about it briefly, then nodded.

"What about us?" I asked.

He looked at Keith and me. "Would you two stop fooling around? Get down from there! And get your clothes on!" Then Stanley looked at Vicky and shook his head. "Kids!"

Yeah, like it was *our* idea to strip so we wouldn't run away.

We gathered all the animals. Then put them in the truck with the animals Vicky had already rescued from the *other* side. It was a bit crowded.

The police were coming down the road to the industrial center.

"They're almost here," I said.

"That road is the only way in or out," Vicky screamed.

"*Oh, my God!*" Keith wailed. "*I'm going to jail!*"

"Calm down, everyone," Stanley said. "There's a trail into the woods on the north side of the building. I'll take you there, in the truck. Then I'll run back. I'll tell the police that the same people must've broken in again. Only this time, they were successful," he said to Vicky with a goofy smile.

"Then what?" I asked.

"You wait in the woods. Till the coast is clear. Then, when the police are gone, you leave."

I looked at Stanley. "Why are you doing this for us?"

"I'm not doing it for you. I'm doing it because it's the right thing to do," he said. "For the animals."

I think I heard Vicky sigh.

ONE LAST THING . . .

In case you wondered . . . Keith passed English.

In fact, his teacher was *very* impressed with his account of *A Tale of Two Cities*. So he ended up getting an A on the project. Which averaged out his English grade to a C+.

Meanwhile, about three months later, I got a letter from Vicky.

It was on fancy paper. From a place called the Harvey Kline Preserve for Mistreated Animals. In *Africa*!

Dear Al,

I now live in the Congo. On a preserve. It's for mistreated animals, and gives them a place to live in peace. We managed to get all the rescued animals here, thanks to the Harvey Kline foundation. They've been really great! And the animals love it here. *Especially* George! (We got her some cool sunglasses with UV protection, and she keeps them on 24/7!) For some reason, she's hooked on Vin Diesel movies. So we have to have "movie night" at least once a week. And it *has* to be a Vin Diesel DVD or George goes nuts.

Oh, and remember Stanley? The security guard? He helped me get the Bosting animals here. And he stayed here too! He just told me to say hi from him. So . . . "Hi" from Stanley. He also told me to tell you he's really calm now. ☺ He says it's because he's so happy. And guess what?! We're getting married!

Thanks for everything, Al! We wouldn't be so happy if it weren't for you and Keith!

If you're ever in the Congo, look us up! We'd
love to have you!

Love, Vicky

Enclosed was a picture of George wearing her red-and-white striped outfit. And a pair of cool, wraparound shades. She was clutching a box of Milk Duds and smiling like crazy.

PENDRAGON

Bobby Pendragon is a seemingly normal fourteen-year-old boy. He has a family, a home, and a possible new girlfriend. But something happens to Bobby that changes his life forever.

HE IS CHOSEN TO DETERMINE THE COURSE OF HUMAN EXISTENCE.

Pulled away from the comfort of his family and suburban home, Bobby is launched into the middle of an immense, interdimensional conflict involving racial tensions, threatened ecosystems, and more. It's a journey of danger and discovery for Bobby, and his success or failure will do nothing less than determine the fate of the world. . . .

Coming Soon: Book Seven: *The Quillan Games*

From Aladdin Paperbacks • Published by Simon & Schuster

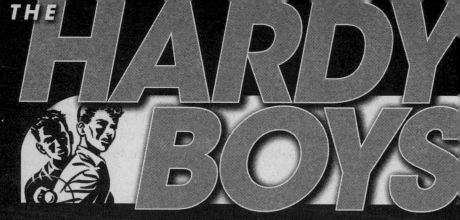

THE HARDY BOYS

UNDERCOVER BROTHERS™

They've got motorcycles,
their cases are ripped from the headlines,
and they work for ATAC:
American Teens Against Crime.

CRIMINALS, BEWARE:
THE HARDY BOYS ARE ON YOUR TRAIL!

Frank and Joe are telling all-new stories of crime,

danger, death-defying stunts, mystery, and teamwork.

Ready? Set? Fire it up!

Imagine a world where families are allowed only two children.

Illegal third children—shadow children—must live in hiding,

for if they are discovered, there is only one punishment:

Death.

Read the Shadow Children series by

MARGARET PETERSON HADDIX